WHITEY'S
NEW SADDLE

Other Avon Camelot Books by
Glen Rounds

WHITEY AND THE COLT-KILLER

WHITEY'S FIRST ROUNDUP

WHITEY TAKES A TRIP

GLEN ROUNDS was born in the Badlands of South Dakota and spent his boyhood on a ranch in Montana. Later, he traveled around the country as a sign painter, cowpuncher, mule skinner, carnival barker, and logger. He studied at the Kansas City Art Institute, the Art Students' League in New York, and served in the U.S. Army. Mr. Rounds is the author of many books for young readers and lives in Southern Pines, North Carolina.

WHITEY's
NEW SADDLE

WHITEY's
NEW SADDLE

Written and Illustrated by

Glen Rounds

AN AVON CAMELOT BOOK

6th grade reading level has been determined by using the Fry Readability Scale.

Based on two stories, *Whitey and the Rustlers* and *Whitey and the Blizzard*, both of which originally appeared in *Story Parade* magazine.

AVON BOOKS
A division of
The Hearst Corporation
959 Eighth Avenue
New York, New York 10019

Copyright 1951, 1952, 1963 by Holiday House, Inc.
Cover illustration by Murray Tinkelman
Published by arrangement with Holiday House, Inc.
Library of Congress Catalog Card Number: 81-20487
ISBN: 0-380-57125-0

First Camelot Printing, May, 1982

Library of Congress Cataloging in Publication Data

Rounds, Glen, 1906-
  Whitey's new saddle.

  (An Avon/Camelot Book)
  "Whitey's new saddle is based on two stories,
Whitey and the rustlers and Whitey and the
blizzard, both of which originally appeared in
Story parade magazine"
  Originally published: New York: Holiday
House, 1963.
  Summary: In trying to earn money for a new
saddle, ten-year-old Whitey endures some
serious mishaps.
  [1. Ranch life—Fiction] I. Title.
PZ7.R761Wj 1982   [Fic]   81-20487
ISBN 0-380-57125-0   AACR2

Printed in the U. S. A.

DON   10 9 8 7 6 5 4 3 2 1

Contents

The Missing Steers

"I DON'T much like the look of that sky," Uncle Torwal remarked as he and Whitey stood on the ranch house porch after breakfast. "The way the barometer is droppin' we could git an early snowstorm."

"Isn't it too early for snow?" Whitey wanted to know.

"We've had blizzards even earlier," Uncle Torwal told him. "Just to be on the safe side I think it might be a good idea to ride out and see how the cattle are doing. If they're on the ridges we'd better drive 'em down onto the bottoms where they'll be out of the wind in case it does storm."

"Yessir," Whitey agreed. "If the wind got behind them they might drift clear down into the Badlands."

So as soon as they'd watered the horses at the windmill tank, they saddled up and rode out—Whitey towards Cedar Springs and Uncle Torwal in the direction of Elk Creek.

In spite of the curious dark clouds banking up in the northwest it was still a fine fall morning. The sun felt warm on Whitey's back, and Old Spot's hooves left a dark trail through the frosty grass. The old horse jogged contentedly along, pointing his ears forward as far as they'd go, then twitching them back. Now and again he'd drop his head and blow softly through his nostrils, making a soft blubbery sound.

Listening to the creaking of his old saddle, Whitey thought about the new one he'd buy after he and Uncle Torwal shipped their beef next month.

He didn't really mind wearing a hand-me-down Stetson of Uncle Torwal's, especially when it had such a fine rattlesnake hatband, for most cowboys wore battered-looking hats when they were working. With a few strips of paper stuffed in the sweatband it stayed on fine. And for the same reason he didn't mind the old boots with the run-over heels.

But this old saddle was something else again. It was a Cogshell with a flat Texas horn, and so old the corners of the skirts were curled up tight, and the strings had long ago been chewed off by calves. Everywhere the stitching was coming undone, and ragged strips of the old sheepskin lining showed in odd places, giving the whole affair the look of a moulting hen. Furthermore, the stirrups were the clumsy iron kind, when the style hereabouts was a neat wooden oxbow pattern. For a long time, Whitey had felt that this saddle spoiled his whole appearance, making him look more like a homesteader than a cowboy.

Of course, when he'd been smaller and first come to live with Uncle Torwal and help him run the Lone Tree Ranch, it hadn't mattered so much. But now that he was past ten years old and practically a top hand he had to think more about the looks of his equipment. People set a lot of store by such things.

So last summer Uncle Torwal had given him two Whiteface calves with the understanding that when they were sold for beef Whitey could use the money to buy a new saddle. Uncle Torwal had even helped him figure out his own cattle brand and sent it off to be registered after they'd put it on the calves with a running iron. It was a fine big squiggle on the ribs with three dots at the end.

The Rattlesnake brand, they called it and

Whitey figured it was about as fine a one as he knew of. He saw no reason why it shouldn't someday be as famous as the old "101." Rattlesnake Ranch sounded good no matter how you said it!

So he rode on for a while, thinking about the time when the Rattlesnake brand would be on hundreds of head of good beef cattle instead of only two, and he'd be able to have

a new saddle every week if he felt like it.

But just when he had started thinking about how fine a Sunday saddle would look, he came on a calf partly bogged in the mud around an old water hole; so he stopped thinking about saddles for a while.

The calf was really in no danger, being plenty strong enough to get out of the mud by himself when he was ready. But Whitey always liked to practice being a first-rate cowboy, and pulling critturs out of mud

was a thing everybody should be handy at.

The old cow was in a nasty humor, bawling and wringing her tail, so he didn't feel it was safe to get down off Spot. And as calves will do, that one had gotten out into the middle of the softest patch of gumbo, so that if Whitey missed his first cast, as he most usually did, he was bound to get his rope all muddy. That never did a throw rope any good. He finally urged Old Spot out onto the mud until he could reach down and drop the loop around the calf's neck.

Taking a hitch around the saddle horn, he turned the old horse, and in no time at all dragged the little crittur out onto solid ground. No cowboy in the country could have done it better, Whitey thought. But when he'd shaken the loop loose and the cow and calf had gone, he found his rope was muddy after all; so he had to get off and find some dry grass to clean it with.

He dried his rope as best he could, carefully coiled it, and strapped it back on his saddle. Then, attracted by the sweet smell of wild plums from a near-by thicket, he left

Spot to crop the rich brown buffalo grass while he went to investigate.

The wind made soft lonely noises overhead but did not disturb the hollow where Whitey squatted. He hated to leave the pleasant place, but he still had his work to do. So, after filling his jacket pockets, he caught the old horse and rode on.

As he came nearer to Cedar Springs he found the cattle grazing in small scattered bunches. They had already begun to drift down into the draws where they were sheltered from the wind; so he left them where they were. But he did examine each bunch, counting them and looking for his two steers.

As he rode close, each animal threw up its head with ears widespread to look and listen; so it was a simple matter to check the earmarks. But nowhere did he find the swallow-tail cut that would identify the two he looked for. And as he checked and counted he became more and more certain that not only were his two missing, but several more besides.

Thinking that perhaps they'd drifted off by themselves somewhere, he looked carefully into all the plum and box elder thickets for some distance in all directions. He even rode up onto the ridge to see if perhaps they'd wandered over onto the other side. But nowhere was there any sign of them; so at last he gave up the search and started back to the ranch.

Riding along under a sky that was now

entirely overcast by cold dark clouds, Whitey tried to figure what had become of his steers. If they were really gone he'd probably have to ride the old saddle for a good while longer.

When he came into the ranch yard he found Uncle Torwal already home. After Whitey had unsaddled Old Spot he spoke about the missing steers.

"That's mighty peculiar," Uncle Torwal said. "There seemed to be a few missing over where I was riding, too. I figured they'd jest drifted down out of sight somewhere, and didn't spend too much time looking for them."

"But if you missed a few from the bunch around Cedar Springs," he went on, "it looks like there is something wrong some-where."

"What do you think might have hap-pened to them?" Whitey asked. "Do you figure it might have been gray wolves?"

"Haven't heard of wolves around here for a long time," Uncle Torwal said. "Be-sides, we'd have found the carcasses. More

likely we'll find they jest drifted away."

"What about cattle rustlers?" Whitey asked.

"Haven't heard much about cattle stealing for a long time, hereabouts," Uncle Torwal told him. "But it does seem odd that they'd drift away in ones and twos."

"Well," Whitey said, "if I don't find mine I won't be able to buy a new saddle for a long time yet."

"If this storm holds off we'll take another look around tomorrow," Uncle Torwal said. "Then if we still can't find any sign of them we'll go in and see if the sheriff knows anything about cattle rustlers working here in Lone Tree County."

The New Spurs

BUT THE NEXT morning when they woke it was snowing steadily, and on the flats only the tips of the sagebrush showed through the soft white mounds. There was no wind; so the flakes lay where they fell, piling high on the tops of the fence posts and along the poles of the corrals.

"No use to go out looking for your steers in this weather," Uncle Torwal remarked as he set the water bucket down and stamped snow off his boots. "That snow's gittin' deeper by the hour."

"I guess you're right," Whitey agreed.

He was disappointed, but there didn't seem to be anything he could do about it.

After they had finished breakfast and washed their dishes, he and Uncle Torwal took their sheepskin coats off the hooks where they'd hung all summer and went out to throw hay over the fence for the stock in the horse pasture.

"We'll chop the ice out of the water troughs later on," Uncle Torwal decided after they'd finished the feeding. "Right now we'd better split up some wood before the wood pile is completely buried."

While they were still working on that a

horseman rode up to the gate and climbed stiffly out of his saddle.

"Looks like Highpockets, Bearpaw Smith's hired man," Uncle Torwal said, as he and Whitey hurried to open the gate.

The horse's muzzle and chest were frosted almost white where his breath had frozen on the tips of the long hairs. And little balls of ice clung to his sides and belly where the snow had partly melted and then refrozen. After they'd given the horse some hay and Highpockets had beaten the snow off his hat brim and the shoulders of his sheepskin, they went into the kitchen to warm up.

"Bearpaw's horse fell on him this morning," the rider told them as he pulled off his boots to warm his feet on the open oven door. "He's got a broken leg and he may have cracked a couple of ribs, too. He wants to be taken to town. It would be a rough trip in the wagon. So he thought maybe with all this snow you could haul him in your bobsled."

"I guess mebbe I could," Uncle Torwal agreed. "Has Doc been out yet?"

"No," Highpockets said. "Bearpaw figured it would be quicker to take him to the Doc. Then he could stay at the Hotel until he was able to get around. I splinted the leg up the best I could and it's not bothering him too much."

"If this storm thickens up I might have to stay overnight in town and come back tomorrow. You think you could take care of things here alone?" Uncle Torwal asked Whitey.

"Sure," Whitey said. "You go ahead. I'll be all right."

"Let's get started, then," Uncle Torwal said to Highpockets. "You go on back and get Bearpaw ready and I'll be along later."

The old bobsled was in the shed where it had been stored all summer. After they'd put half a dozen bricks in the oven to heat, Whitey and Uncle Torwal piled robes and quilts on top of a deep layer of hay in the bottom of the box. By the time they'd finished that and harnessed the team, the bricks were ready to be wrapped in gunny sacks and put down in the pile of hay.

"Now mind what I say, Bub," Uncle Torwal said as he arranged his big buffalo coat around him on the seat of the bobsled and gathered up the lines. "Don't go far from the buildings here unless it clears up some. The way the barometer is falling this snow could turn into a blizzard without half trying!"

Whitey looked at the fine dry snow that had been falling steadily all over Lone Tree County since the night before, and saw the air was still with no sign of wind.

"It doesn't look like it was going to get much worse," he said.

"Mebbe it won't," Uncle Torwal agreed, "but with all this fine snow on the ground, if the wind come up good and brisk you'd not be able to see your hand in front of your face inside ten minutes. But you look after the ranch, and I'll be back tonight or some time tomorrow. So long, now." And he spoke to the horses and drove out of the ranch yard.

Whitey closed the gate after him, and stood watching until the team and sled were hidden by the falling snow. Then he turned back to the ranch yard, deciding what should be done next.

Altogether he felt pretty much like a full-fledged cowboy, and Uncle Torwal almost never treated him like anything else. Still, he would be glad when he was big enough to go into Lone Tree, to Mr. Highwater Johnson's Stockmen's Clothing Store and buy him a Stetson and a pair of boots, all brand-new, and maybe not have to take the smallest size, either.

He wished they had a lot of cattle to look after and maybe a corral full of horses to be broken to ride, while Uncle Torwal was gone.

However, there were still chores to be done, so Whitey chopped ice out of the water trough and pumped water for the stock. Then he filled the mangers with hay from the stacks in the stackyard. After that he carried wood into the kitchen.

By the time he'd finished those things it was almost noon, so he got a hammer and the big butcher knife and chopped a steak off the quarter of beef hanging frozen outside the door. After he'd eaten and washed his plate and the skillet, he sat down to work a little on the fancy hackamore noseband he was braiding from rawhide and old boot leather.

But he soon gave that up and got out the mail-order catalogue, turning to the picture of the saddle he planned to order when he got the money for his beef. On the same page was a picture of the spurs he'd ordered last week, so as to have them ready to wear with his new saddle when he did get it.

He'd saved his money for a long time, waiting to send for those spurs. They had long gooseneck shanks, and dollar rowells, with a bright chain that went under the instep. But the finest thing about them was the two little bells that hung just by the outside buckle on each spur.

They would be fine to wear when he and Uncle Torwal went into Lone Tree of a Saturday. They would jingle wonderfully

when he walked on the wooden sidewalks,
or when he went into the stores.

The more Whitey thought about it now,
the more certain he was that those spurs
were over in the mailbox right now. The
mail carrier made his trip twice a week, and
yesterday afternoon had been mail day. It
just happened that he and Uncle Torwal
had forgotten to go after the mail last night.

Whitey scratched a hole in the thick frost
on the window and looked out. It was a little over two miles out to the main road
where the mailbox was, and Uncle Torwal
had told him not to go far away unless the
weather cleared.

However, it looked to him like the snow
was already thinning just the least little bit.

Rattlesnake Butte, less than half a mile away, was just a faint blur through the snow, but he was sure he could see it a little plainer than he had when Uncle Torwal was leaving. Of course, that wasn't exactly clear weather, but on the other hand, Uncle Torwal hadn't said just how clear the weather should be before he went out, and there still was no sign of wind.

The more he thought about it, the more sure he was that it'd be all right for him to go out to the mailbox to get his spurs. He'd have to walk, because Old Spot had slipped on some ice the day before and was a little lame, but if he took his .22 rifle he might get a couple of rabbits or maybe even a coyote on the way.

Each time he looked out of the clear place he'd scratched in the frost on the window he thought the snow was thinning a little more. So at last he made his mind up to go.

In almost no time he had his heavy sheepskin coat on and a scarf tied over his ears. At the last minute he decided to put his big four-buckle overshoes on over his boots. Then he picked up his rifle and started out.

As soon as he walked away from the house, Whitey saw that the snow was still falling steadily after all, and lay on the ground almost boot-top deep. It fell softly as feathers, muffling all sounds. A few yards off, fences and buildings seemed to melt into the soft gray and there was no difference between ground and sky.

But this didn't bother Whitey, for he felt perfectly able to find his way. And the way the snow and the light changed the shapes of things gave him the feeling of exploring strange country no one had ever seen before.

Small birds in flocks of ten or twenty rustled around under the sagebrush or flew quickly from one place to another, complaining uneasily.

The first half-mile he was in the big horse pasture, but when he came to that fence and crawled through he had to go straight across the open flat, where there were neither trees nor fences for miles in any direction.

He saw some rabbits, and once a big brown owl sailed past, skimming so low his wingtips now and again left marks in the soft snow.

Whitey almost ran the last quarter of a mile, stumbling and sliding through the soft snow, in his hurry to see if his spurs were really there. He got to the mailbox without

difficulty, and threw down two rabbits he'd shot on the way.

When he opened the big wooden box standing on its posts, he saw the mailsack with Uncle Torwal's name stenciled on the side. It didn't seem to be bulging as it should if his spurs were in it, but he untied the string and started taking the mail out to be sure.

There were four or five copies of Uncle Torwal's *Stockman's Gazette,* and under them was a new saddle catalogue. In the very bottom he felt a little package. It seemed too small to be spurs, but when he got it out of the mailsack he found it was addressed to him, after all.

He stuffed the rest of the mail back in the sack, along with the two rabbits, and slung the sack over his shoulders so he'd have his hands free as he started back towards the ranch. Carrying his rifle under his arm, he broke the strings and tore the paper wrappings off the box.

Inside, nested in crumpled paper, were the spurs, looking even more beautiful than they had in the catalogue. The straps were rich brown leather with a handsome design stamped onto them, and the bells, when he shook them, had a fine silvery tone.

Blizzard

WHITEY had been stumbling along through the snow for some time, with eyes for nothing but his fine new spurs, when he suddenly noticed the wind was blowing against his face, and stopped to look around. The snow had thickened until he could see only a little way in any direction, and the wind was already picking more off the ground and whirling it into the air in blinding clouds. The mailbox behind him was already hidden and, as he stood watching,

his tracks were blown full of snow and disappeared.

This was the thing Uncle Torwal had
warned him about. However, Whitey wasn't
worried, for all he had to do was walk
straight ahead and he'd soon come to the
pasture fence, and he could follow it right
on around to the corrals. But he felt it wasn't
a good idea to waste any more time; so he
stuffed the spurs back into the mailsack and
hurried ahead, bowing his head to protect
his face from the beating of the snow.

Before he'd gone any great distance the
wind was blowing full force, and seemed to
push and shove at him from all sides. It roared
and cracked until his ears rang with it. His
breath froze on the edges of his coat collar

and gathered in white frost on his eyelashes and brows. The powdery fine snow whipped into his eyes and nose until it was almost impossible to see or breathe.

But there was no shelter near. There was nothing for him to do but keep walking, and hope he could keep his direction by the feel of the wind on his face. He'd heard stories of people lost in storms who'd wandered around in circles without knowing it.

He had been walking a long time and was just beginning to wonder if maybe he had somehow missed his way, when he ran right into the barbed wire. He walked against it without seeing it, and the shock threw him off balance so that he fell floundering in the snow, dropping his rifle. Picking himself up, he felt around until he found the gun, then held onto the wire while he caught his breath.

Turning his back to the wind, he took off his mittens to warm his nose and cheeks, feeling pretty well pleased with himself for getting safely to the fence. It would never have done to have gotten lost in the blizzard right after Uncle Torwal had warned him against that very thing!

Just before he turned to start hand over hand along the wire, the driving snow thinned enough for him to see that this wasn't the pasture fence after all. It was only a small stackyard fence, one of several built out on the open flats to keep range stock away from the stacks of wild hay the ranchers cut for winter feed. He knew then that he was lost.

If there had still been hay in the stackyard he might have burrowed into it and waited out the storm. But the ground inside the fence was bare; so there was nothing for him to do but go on.

By keeping the wind in his face as he walked he would still be able to find the pasture fence. The trouble was to tell which direction the wind was coming from, for it whipped and eddied until it seemed to come from first one way, and then another.

However, he would freeze for sure if he stayed where he was; so he started out again. This time he took care to walk straight ahead, but after a long time he knew that in spite of himself he had drifted off his straight line.

He had a hard time then, keeping himself

from getting panicky and running to find some landmark that looked familiar. But this was one of the things that the cowboys had always spoken of that a lost person must avoid at all costs. So every little way he made himself stop and stand still, swinging his arms to keep warm while he caught his breath.

Starting ahead after one of these stops, he

suddenly felt the ground give way under his feet, and the next thing he knew he had fallen several feet, landing up to his neck in soft snow. Overhead he could see a circle of light, and when he felt around he found solid walls of earth on two sides of him.

He'd fallen into one of the deep narrow washouts common in that country. The walls were higher than his head and too steep to climb, while the head-high drifts blocked his way in the other directions.

He could hear the wind booming just over-head, and dry fine snow sifted steadily down into the hole where he stood. Getting back up onto the flat was going to be a problem.

Whitey tried to remember all the things he'd heard Uncle Torwal and the other old-timers tell about the ways men had gotten themselves out of this predicament and that. But somehow none of the stories had ever seemed to have been about fellows falling in-to washouts during blizzards.

He got out his pocketknife and, after some difficulty getting the blade open with his numb fingers, he started trying to cut steps in the steep bank. It was hard, slow work, digging at the frozen dirt with the small blade, and when he had gotten a couple of steps cut he found that the bank sloped inwards. So he slipped and fell back when he tried to climb up.

As he scrabbled about in the snow trying to regain his feet, he uncovered what appeared to be the corner of a fresh cowhide. After considerable pulling, and digging with his hands, he finally dug out three roughly-rolled hides which had been carelessly hidden by caving part of the bank onto them. The covering of dirt had kept them from freezing so that he was able to unroll them enough to find what brands they carried.

Two were marked with his Rattlesnake

brand, and the other with Uncle Torwal's Lone Tree!

There went his hopes for a new saddle!

Whitey knew how the rustlers worked, going out to the range in trucks. At dusk they'd butcher two or three fat steers they'd spotted during the afternoon, bury the hides, and have the meat sold in another county before the rancher even suspected his stock was missing.

A sudden heavier gust of wind tumbled a flurry of snow into the washout, reminding Whitey that it was time he started finding a way back onto the flat. The problem of the rustlers would have to wait.

Getting to his feet, he bumped against the rifle, which he had dropped when he fell. Now it occurred to him that if he could brace it across the gully some way, he'd have a step to climb up on.

He found that the rifle was considerably longer than the distance between the walls; so he dug another hole on the opposite side

from the steps, and about level with the high-
est one. He jammed the muzzle in one hole,

and wedged the butt in another on the other side. Carefully trying his weight on it, he found it was solid enough to hold him; so all he had to do was get his feet up on it, if he could.

That took some doing, however, in the narrow space, bundled up as he was and with the mailsack still slung over his shoulder. But he managed to get his chest across the rifle, then by squirming and twisting he got a knee across, and finally braced his foot on the gun stock against the wall. After that he carefully straightened up, supporting himself against the sides with his hands until he had both feet firmly braced on either end of the rifle.

With his head and shoulders above the

level of the ground it was no great job to pull himself up and roll out onto the snow.

While he was standing there, pleased to be on solid ground again, stamping his feet and beating his arms to warm himself, a jack rabbit passed within a few feet of him. It hurried along as silently as a gray shadow, almost invisible in the snow. As Whitey watched it disappear in the storm he wondered where it could be going—probably to shelter.

Taking a few steps in the direction of the rabbit's tracks, he felt a deep, worn cattle path under his feet. The chances were good that it led either to shelter or a fence he could follow.

It was only in scattered places that the wind had cleared the new snow off so he could see the little path. The rest of the time he had to scrape around with his feet every step to find it.

After what seemed like ages to Whitey, the trail suddenly dipped over a bank and disappeared in deep snowdrifts. Before he could catch himself, he slipped and rolled to the bottom. When he picked himself up, he found he was in a deep draw, and that the drifts were too deep for him to find the path again. But at least he'd gotten off the flats.

It wasn't long before he found that, even though he was protected from the wind, traveling down the draw was going to be more difficult than he'd thought. The drifts were so deep he struggled along in snow to his waist much of the time, and the fine stuff powdered down from above so thickly he could hardly get his breath.

Once or twice he thought about throwing away the mailsack, after he'd put his new spurs in his pocket of course, but always he figured the two rabbits might come in handy. The rest of the mail wasn't heavy enough to make any difference; so he left it slung on his back.

He knew he'd freeze in a hurry if he stopped moving, and kept telling himself that he'd just go around one more bend before he stopped. And then he went around another, and finally another, until he couldn't seem to remember how many he'd passed.

When he bumped into a big cottonwood tree standing squarely in his path he stopped and leaned against it to rest and catch his breath. It wasn't until he straightened up, ready to move on, that he noticed the pieces of board nailed to the trunk—and then for the first time he knew where he was. This was the old Owls' Nest Tree. Somebody years before had nailed boards to the trunk to make a ladder to the nest where the pair of great horned owls raised two young ones every year. And less than a hundred yards

down the draw there was an old shack the hay crews sometimes used.

Now that he was close to shelter Whitey forgot his tiredness. He went confidently ahead, keeping close to the bank and counting his steps so he'd know if he passed the shack without seeing it in the swirling snow.

Feeling his way along the wall, he floundered through the deep drifts until he found the door, hanging crookedly from one hinge, and squeezed his way inside.

While his eyes adjusted themselves to the gloom Whitey leaned against the wall, catching his breath and listening to the storm outside.

Some snow had sifted into the shack and in places was several inches deep. But after his long struggle against the beating of the wind and the smothering swirling snow, this place seemed safe and comfortable. Even so, he realized he would quickly chill, now that he wasn't moving, unless he managed to get a fire started.

Against one wall there was a litter of old broken pieces of lumber and wooden boxes. Using one of the boards for a shovel, he soon scraped a patch of the dirt floor clear in the most sheltered corner. Then he got his jack-knife opened and started whittling kindling sticks, setting them in a teepee-shaped stack. His matches were in an empty shotgun shell he always carried in his sheepskin pocket.

As soon as the fine feathery shavings caught and began to blaze, he carefully added larger sticks, one at a time, until his little fire was burning well.

Unbuttoning his heavy coat and taking off his mittens, he huddled over the fire, soaking up the warmth. Backed into the corner as he was, no drafts could reach him. Some of the smoke found its way out through cracks and holes up near the roof but most of it eddied about inside, making his eyes smart, and gusts outside occasionally sent fine snow sifting down inside his collar. But these were small things and he didn't mind them too much.

When Whitey had warmed himself he began a more careful examination of the place. In another corner he found more bits of lumber, as well as three old fence posts. He had no axe to chop them up with, but he could use them Indian fashion: putting one end in the fire and shoving them forward a little at a time as they burned away. By burning one at a time they'd easily last the night through if he was careful.

Having taken care of the fuel problem, Whitey set about making his corner more comfortable. A few pieces of board to sit on would keep the chill of the frozen ground away from him. And, kicking into a drift in another corner, he discovered an old piece of heavy canvas. It was dirty and stained, but he propped it up in the corner with some sticks and made a small tent that would keep the snow off and trap more of the heat from the little fire.

Arranging himself as comfortably as possible in his shelter, Whitey built up the fire and thought about his situation. This storm would keep Uncle Torwal in town; so he wouldn't be worrying about where he was.

And with shelter and wood enough to last the night he was in no real danger. But he was hungry.

That reminded him of the rabbits in the mailsack. Getting his knife out again, it took only a few minutes to skin and dress them. Now all he needed was a piece of wire to make a grill to broil the meat on.

Searching the place again, he noticed that three boxes in the middle of the room were arranged like a table and two chairs. Dusting the snow off the larger one, he found a checkerboard drawn in pencil on the top. Puzzled by that, he scraped around in the snow on the floor and found some homemade checker pieces—as well as two fairly new western story magazines. Somebody had spent some time in the place quite lately, reading and playing checkers.

As far as Whitey knew, no hay crews had been around here for a year or more. Besides, hay crews seldom had time to read magazines or to play games.

Finding the wire he needed, Whitey crawled back into his tent and started cooking his rabbit. The smell of the roasting meat, sizzling and spitting above the little fire, drove all other thoughts out of his mind. After he'd eaten the meat and sucked the bones, the warmth and the sound of the storm made him drowsy.

Pulling the old canvas close about him, he huddled over the tiny fire, rousing now and again to add small scraps of wood or to pull the fence post forward a little as the end burned away. Occasionally he dozed, but the cold always woke him before the fire went completely out.

It was sometime near morning when he realized he was no longer hearing the wind. Getting stiffly to his feet, he shoved the door open a crack and looked out. The storm had stopped and the stars were shining. Quickly gathering up the mailsack, he squeezed outside and floundered through the drifts between the shack and the top of the bank.

Once he was out of the draw and up on the flats the walking wasn't difficult, and the starlight on the snow was bright enough to make traveling easy.

After Whitey had gotten back home and

rebuilt the fire in the stove he took the new spurs out of the mailsack and tried them on. Tired as he was, he spent a while walking about the warm kitchen to hear the tinkling of the little silver bells. He saw no chance now of getting a new saddle, but he felt that having the fanciest spurs in Lone Tree County was probably the next best thing!

The Rustlers

BY THE TIME Whitey had fixed himself some breakfast the sun had come up. The light on the new snow was blinding, and the air sparkled with falling frost crystals. For a while he watched the saddle horses warming themselves in the sunshine reflected from the stable wall, then he started the morning chores. Before he'd finished, Uncle Torwal drove in.

"Everything go all right here?" he asked, as they unhitched the horses.

"Yessir," Whitey told him. "And I found out for sure that the rustlers are getting our steers."

"You did?" Uncle Torwal asked.

"Yessir, I dug up three fresh hides that had been buried in a washout over towards the old Owls' Nest Tree," Whitey told him. Then, before Uncle Torwal could ask how he'd happened to be out in the storm, he went on. "I'd been over for the mail when the wind came up, so I decided to stay in that old shack until it cleared."

Uncle Torwal figured there was probably more to the story than he'd been told, but everything seemed to have turned out all right; so he said nothing about it. And that suited Whitey just fine. Later on he'd tell

Uncle Torwal the whole story, but just now didn't seem to be the right time.

"Were the brands cut out?" Uncle Torwal wanted to know.

For usually rustlers cut the brand out and burn it before burying the hide.

"Reckon they must have been careless this time. One was a Lone Tree steer and the other two were Rattlesnake brand."

"Got both yours, did they?" Uncle Torwal said, and whistled. "That was tough goin', cleanin' out your whole spread."

"Yeah, that's a fact," Whitey said. "Looks like I'll ride my old hull a while longer."

He led Spot into the stable so Uncle Torwal wouldn't see how badly he really did feel.

They didn't say much as they finished the chores and ate dinner, but afterwards, as they sat by the stove warming their feet, Uncle Torwal spoke up.

"Reckon we might as well ride in and see the sheriff. Now that we know for sure that rustlers are working around here, maybe we can figure out something."

"I sure hope so," Whitey said. "They did me out of a new saddle and I'd surely like to catch them!"

When they got to town they tied their horses and walked into the sheriff's office. Mr. Hairpants Hagadorn, the sheriff, shook hands with them while Mr. Fort Worth Wilkerson, the deputy sheriff, dragged out chairs.

After some polite talk of this and that, Uncle Torwal told the sheriff what Whitey had found.

"This is the first time we've had any proof," the sheriff said, "but there's been a lot of complaints of missin' beef critturs all up and down the valley."

"How you reckon they get in and out of the valley without anyone knowing?" Uncle Torwal said after a little.

"I been considering that myself," the sheriff told him. "They have to come through here or through Hill City to get in or out, and we've been watchin' both places close, yet nobody has seen any strangers or strange truck."

"I wish we could catch them," Whitey spoke up. "I was goin' to get a new saddle with the money from the steers they got of mine!"

"Well, maybe you can figure how to catch them and use your share of the reward money for that saddle," the sheriff told him.

At the mention of REWARD Whitey stopped looking at the posters and notices tacked over the sheriff's desk and brightened right up.

"You mean there's a reward for those rustlers?" he asked.

"Sure," the sheriff told him. "I got the notice around here somewhere."

After some more talk they shook hands with the sheriff, the deputy sheriff, and a man who had wandered into the office looking for a place to sit down, and rode off towards the ranch.

As they rode along Whitey thought about

that reward and tried to figure out some way he could earn it. It seemed to him that to get money enough for a new saddle by trapping rustlers was even better than getting it by selling cattle.

"Uncle Torwal!" he said, suddenly remembering something. "Somebody has been using that old shack by the Owls' Nest Tree. I found a checkerboard and a couple of magazines when I was there. Could it be the rustlers, do you suppose?"

Uncle Torwal thought a while. "It could be, mebbe," he said. "There used to be an old road through there that went down into the Box Elder road. They might come in early when no one would notice them and hide the truck in the draw until dusk."

"Why don't we lay for them when they come back?" Whitey asked, thinking of the reward and his new saddle.

"Well, Bub, they might not come back. Those dudes are pretty smart an' don't often work the same place twice. That's why they're so hard to catch." After seeing how Whitey's face fell, he went on, "On the other hand, with a hideout like that they might feel safe for a while longer. From all the talk of missin' cattle in the valley, they must have made several trips already."

"Tell you what," Uncle Torwal said, as they neared the ranch. "We might take turns watchin' that place for a while, jest in case they did come back."

"Yessir!" Whitey agreed. "We'll catch

'em coming in and collect the rewards!''

"We don't want to bother 'em coming in," Torwal corrected him. "We jest want to know when they get there so we'll have time to call the sheriff to catch 'em going out with the meat in the truck for evidence."

Whitey still favored capturing the rustlers without interference from the sheriff, but he said nothing about it. He was bound he'd get that saddle the rustlers had done him out of, and even part of the reward would be enough.

"I'll take my blankets and go out right away to watch for them," he said.

"You won't need any blankets," Uncle Torwal told him. "Those fellers probably come in about the middle of the afternoon so they'll be able to locate the critturs they want before dusk. Besides, there's no need to start watching until this snow is gone."

The next morning when Whitey and Uncle Torwal got up they found that the weather had turned warm again, and the snow was already disappearing almost as fast as it had fallen. The eaves of the ranch house were dripping. Out on the flats the tops of the sagebrush showed dark above the surface of the rapidly settling snow.

"Another day of this and we can start watching for the rustlers to come back," Uncle Torwal remarked, as he whittled shavings to start the fire in the cookstove.

"Yessir, this looks like it would go in a hurry," Whitey agreed as he picked up the water buckets and headed for the well.

When they'd finished the morning's chores Uncle Torwal decided to change the shoes on his saddle horse. Whitey saddled Old Spot and went to get his rifle out of the washout.

By noon next day the snow was nearly all gone, although the ground was still wet and muddy under foot. Whitey decided it was time to start watching for the rustlers.

As he got ready to ride out, Uncle Torwal spoke up. "If they don't show up today we'll take turns watching for a few days."

"I don't want anyone to take turns," Whitey hollered. "I'm the one they cleaned out, and I'll watch every day."

So every afternoon for almost a week he

rode out to a small butte where he could watch the road to the old shack. He carefully hid Spot in a plum thicket and then crawled Indian fashion to the top of the butte, and lay

hidden in the sagebrush like some old-time scout. But nothing happened, and he began to believe the rustlers had deserted the valley.

Then one afternoon he was just tying Old Spot in the thicket when he heard a truck motor. He hurried up the slope to his lookout and the sound was plainer there. It was a powerful motor, and working hard. Soon a big closed truck came in sight, moving cautiously down the old road. It disappeared into the draw by the shack and the motor stopped.

It was rustlers, sure enough!

Whitey had been complaining to himself because Uncle Torwal wouldn't let him bring his rifle and capture the rustlers singlehanded, but tonight he thought of nothing but getting back to the ranch as soon as possible to tell Uncle Torwal and get word to the sheriff. He agreed now that it was really the sheriff's business to deal with such people.

Spot got the surprise of his life when Whitey clapped spurs and quirt onto him! He couldn't remember the last time he'd traveled faster than a trot. But as this seemed to be a special occasion he did his best, and before long Whitey and Uncle Torwal were sitting out by the road waiting for the sheriff and his deputies to come by and pick them up.

The word had spread, and by the time the sheriff got there, ranchers and cowboys from up and down the valley had gathered. Most of them carried rifles on their saddles, or pis-

tols in their belts. Rustlers were not popular thereabouts, and Whitey was looking forward to a right exciting time when they caught up with them.

When the sheriff came, just before dusk,

they all rode together towards the shack where the truck had been hidden. Whitey had been afraid someone would tell him to stay behind, but no one did and he rode along with the others.

The rustlers were gone when they got there. But Sheriff Hagadorn said that was all right—as they had to come back this way after they'd finished butchering.

The men had all been concealed in the plum thickets on either side of the road for what seemed a mighty long time to Whitey, when they heard the rustlers coming back.

"This is when the bullets start to fly!" Whitey thought, as the sheriff stepped out into the light of the truck and held up his hand.

But the truck stopped without protest. Deputies and ranch men turned on flashlights and swarmed all round it. Four weasely-looking men climbed carefully out and stood with their hands raised while they and the truck were searched.

"There's plenty beef in here!" a deputy hollered.

"All right!" the sheriff answered. "One of you drive the truck along behind me, and we'll haul these gents down to our jail for a spell."

The rustlers didn't say anything, except to sort of mutter to themselves. They didn't look like the tough fellows Whitey had been picturing in his mind. They weren't wearing gun belts, and they didn't talk back to the sheriff. Worst of all, they wore bib overalls, like farmers, and one even had on a straw hat and plow shoes! Whitey was mighty disappointed in them.

Early next morning Whitey and Uncle Torwal went to town, and Mr. Bugeye Beasly, editor of the *Lone Tree Eagle,* interviewed Whitey.

The reward turned out to be only fifty dollars, and that divided six ways, so there was not enough to buy the saddle with. Whitey had built his hopes so high on that reward, that he felt mighty bad for a few days.

But after reading what Mr. Beasly wrote about him in the paper, how his alertness had helped make Lone Tree County free of rustlers and the like, he sort of got used to the idea of getting along with the old saddle another year.

Then one morning Uncle Torwal told him, "We gotta go to town this morning, Bub. Sheriff said something about wanting to see you."

All the way into town Whitey wondered what the sheriff could want. Maybe he wanted to make him a deputy or something. He imagined this and that, but never thought of the real answer.

After some talk the sheriff pointed to a grain sack on the floor and told Whitey, "Feller left that here an' told me to give it to you."

Whitey opened it up and inside was a brand-new saddle, the decorations hand-tooled, the whangleather tie strings shining bright yellow, the sheepskin lining bright and clean, and the whole thing smelling of neat's foot oil and new leather. It was the most beautiful saddle Whitey had ever seen.

On the back of the cantle was a small silver

plate he'd missed at first. It was engraved:

To Whitey for Service in Ridding
Lone Tree County of Rustlers
From the Lone Tree Stockmen's Ass'n.

Whitey couldn't think of anything to say, so he just grinned and carried the saddle out to try how it looked on Spot.

The story of a special friendship between a boy and a girl . . .

Katherine Paterson
BRIDGE TO TERABITHIA
Illustrated by Donna Diamond

Fifth-grader Jess Aarons secretly longs to be an artist but outwardly works at becoming the fastest runner in his class. Jess is beaten in the first race of the year by newcomer Leslie Burke and the two become fast friends. They create an imaginary kingdom, Terabithia, where none of their enemies—bullying schoolmates, Jess' four sisters, Leslie's imaginary foes or Jess' fears—can defeat them. Leslie opens worlds of art and literature to Jess and changes him forever, helping him to cope with an unexpected and tragic event that shatters his life.

WINNER OF THE NEWBERY AWARD
An Avon Camelot Book   55301 • $1.95